AF582224

INSIGHT PUBLICA

Nadakkave, Kozhikode, Kerala
Tel:0495–4020666
www.insightpublica.com
e-mail: insightpublica@gmail.com

Stories for Children

Leo Tolstoy

The Elephant

Alexander Kuprin

Insight Publica Facsimile Edition: July 2020

ISBN 978-93-90355-53-2

STORIES FOR CHILDREN

Leo Tolstoy

THE ELEPHANT

Alexander Kuprin

(Page No. 49-72)

Those fantastic Soviet Books Again

All of us still have those fond memories of the books from the erstwhile Soviet Union, which were once extensively circuated here, in Kerala - books of fabulous tales, riveting scientific facts and enchanting illustrations which stole the readers' hearts. They left in us an indelible impression and an unforgettable reading experience. An experience still ever-green in us, Malayali diaspora.

As the Union got dissolved, those charming books of tales too vanished, turning them into cherished memories of nostalgia. Yet, readers have relentlessly been looking for those inimitable books. That was why we, the INSIGHT PUBLICA, published a few of them in the same mode. We are grateful and glad to say that readers whole-heartedly backed us in realizing the project.

During the execution of our mission,we could fathom the depth and breadth of a great nation's remarkable literary project. Those sublime Soviet stories traversed in translation into many a nation and many a language. Those books were ubiquitous-not as merchandise, but as products of culture.

The fantastic bolstering that INSIGHT PUBLICA could get is the impetus that drove us daringly to undertake the mission of reprinting and republishing those Soviet works in Indian languages.

You readers need not anymore be discontented with the scanned copies of these books. INSIGHT PUBLICA will help reach into your hands those very books with the same freshness and warmth.

Let us present you again those fantastic Soviet Stories with humility and pride.

Sumesh Insight

LEV TOLSTOI

STORIES FOR CHILDREN

CONTENTS

THE KITTEN

There were once a brother and a sister named Vasya and Katya, and they had a cat. In the spring the cat disappeared. The children looked for it everywhere, but could not find it.

One day they were playing near the barn and heard the meowing of tiny voices overhead. Vasya climbed the ladder to the hayloft.

Katya stood below and kept asking, "Find them? Did you find them?"

But Vasya did not reply. At last, he shouted, "I found them! It's our cat. And she has kittens. They're so cute. Come up here, quick."

Katya ran home, got some milk and took it back for the cat.

There were five kittens. When they grew a little older and began coming out of the corner where they had been born the children chose one for themselves, a gray kitten with white paws, and brought it home. Their mother gave away the other kittens, but left this one for the children. The children fed it, played with it and let it sleep on their beds.

One day the children went out to play on the road and took the kitten along.

The wind was blowing bits of straw along the road. The kitten

played with the straw, and the children laughed as they watched it. Then they came upon some sorrel growing by the roadside. They went off to pick it and forgot all about the kitten.

Suddenly they heard someone shouting: "Back! Back! " and saw a hunter riding towards them with his two hounds running on ahead. The dogs had spotted the kitten and wanted to catch it. The silly kitten crouched, arched its back and stared at the dogs instead of running away.

The hounds frightened Katya. She screamed and ran away. But Vasya made a dash for the kitten and reached it just as the hounds did.

The dogs were about to snatch the kitten, but Vasya flopped down on the road and shielded the kitten with his body.

Then the hunter came galloping up and chased off his dogs. Vasya brought the kitten home and never took it out to the fields again.

THE GIRL AND THE MUSHROOMS

Two girls were returning from the woods with their baskets full of mushrooms.

They had to cross the railroad tracks.

They thought the train was far away, climbed the embankment and began stepping over the rails.

Suddenly, they heard the sound of the locomotive. The elder girl darted back, but the younger one ran on across the rails.

The elder girl shouted to her sister, "Don't turn back! "

But the train was so close and was making so much noise that the younger girl did not hear her. She thought her sister wanted her to run back. She ran back across the rails, tripped, dropped her basket and began gathering up the mushrooms.

The train was now very close. The engineer pulled the whistle as hard as he could.

The elder girl shouted, "Leave the mushrooms! " But the little girl thought she was telling her to gather up the mushrooms and so kept bending over for them.

The engineer could not stop the train in time. The train whistle shrieked, and the train rolled on over the girl.

The elder girl screamed and sobbed. All the passengers looked out of the car windows, while the conductor ran to the far end of the train to see what had happened to the girl.

When the train had passed the spot, everyone saw the little girl lying face-down between the rails. She was lying very still.

Then she raised her head, got up on her knees, gathered up her mushrooms and ran back to her sister.

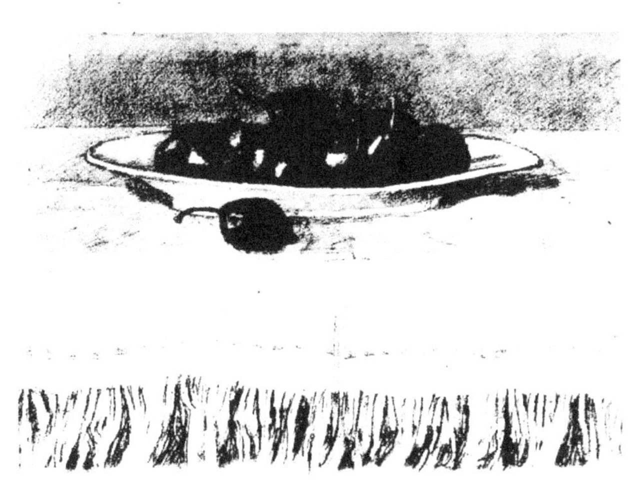

THE PLUM PIT

Mother bought some plums for the children's dessert. The plums were on a plate. Vanya had never tasted a plum and kept sniffing them. He liked the looks of them very much. He wanted so to try them. He kept walking past the plate. When there was no one in the room, the temptation became too great. He snatched a plum and ate it. Mother counted the plums before dinner and saw that one was missing. She told Father.

At dinner Father said, "Did anyone eat a plum, children?"

They all replied:

"No."

Vanya became as red as a beet. He, too, said, "No, I didn't."

Then Father said, "It was not nice of one of you to have eaten it. But that does not matter now. What does is that there are pits in the plums, and if someone does not know how to eat a plum and swallows the pit, he will die the next day. That is what I am so afraid of."

Vanya turned pale and said, "Oh, I threw the pit out of the window."

Then everyone laughed, but Vanya burst into tears.

THE LITTLE BIRD

It was Seryozha's birthday, and he received many presents: tops, hobby-horses and picture books. But the best gift of all was from his uncle. It was a net for catching birds.

A little board was attached to a frame on which a net was stretched. Grain was sprinkled on the board, and then the net was set out in the yard. When a bird flew up and perched on the board, the board would turn over and the net would fall.

Seryozha was so happy he came running to his mother to show her his net.

His mother said, "It's not a nice toy at all. What do you want with little birds? Why do you want to torment them?"

"I'll put them in cages. They'll sing, and I'll feed them."

Seryozha got some grain, sprinkled it on the little board and set the net out in the garden. He stood next to it, waiting for birds to come flying down. But the birds were afraid of him and did not come near the net.

Seryozha went in to dinner and left the net in the garden. When he came to look at it after dinner he saw that the net had fallen and a little bird was thrashing about under it. Seryozha was very excited. He caught the bird and took it into the house.

"Look, Mamma! I've caught a bird. It must be a nightingale. Oh, how fast its heart is beating."

His mother said, "It's a siskin. Don't torment it. Let it go."

"No, I'll feed it and care for it."

Seryozha put the siskin in a cage, and for two days he fed it grain, changed its water and cleaned the cage. On the third day he forgot about the siskin and did not change its water.

Then his mother said to him, "See? You forgot all about your little bird. I think you had better let it go."

"No, I won't forget. I'll give it some fresh water now and clean the cage."

Seryozha stuck his hand into the cage and began cleaning it, but the siskin became frightened and beat its wings against the cage. Seryozha cleaned the cage out and went for water.

His mother saw that he had forgotten to close the little door and called after him, "Close the cage door, Seryozha, or your bird might fly out and hurt itself."

No sooner had she said this than the siskin found the door, spread its wings happily and flew across the room to the window. But it did not see the glass pane. It hit the pane and fell to the windowsill.

Seryozha came running, picked up the little bird and took it back to the cage. The siskin was alive, but it lay on its breast with its little wings spread out and was breathing jerkily. Seryozha began to cry.

"Mamma! What'll I do?"

"There's nothing you can do now."

Seryozha did not leave the room that day. He kept gazing at the siskin. The siskin lay on its breast as before, breathing jerkily. When Seryozha went to bed that night the siskin was still alive. Seryozha could not fall asleep for a long while. No sooner would he close his eyes than he would imagine the siskin lying there, gasping for breath.

When Seryozha went up to the cage the next morning he saw the siskin lying on its back with its legs curled up. It was dead.

Never again did Seryozha catch another bird.

THE LIAR

A shepherd boy was out with his flock. Once he decided to shout, as though he had seen a wolf, "Help! A wolf! A wolf! "

The village men came running and saw that he had tricked them. He did this two or three times more. Then it so happened that a wolf really did attack the flock.

The boy began to shout, "Come! Hurry! It's a wolf! "

The village men decided that he was tricking them again and paid no attention to him.

The wolf saw he need fear no one and killed the whole flock.

TWO FRIENDS

Two friends were walking through the forest when a bear attacked them. One turned and fled. He climbed a tree and sat there, while the other remained on the road. There was nothing for him to do but fall to the ground and play dead.

The bear came up to him and sniffed. The man even stopped breathing.

The bear sniffed his face, decided he was dead and lumbered off.

When the bear was gone the other man climbed down and said with a smile, "What did the bear whisper in your ear?"

"It said that someone who deserts his friend in time of danger is not a good person at all."

THE SWAN

A flock of swans was flying south from the cold lands in the north. The swans were flying across the sea. They had flown over the water a day and a night, and a second day and a second night, never stopping to rest. There was a full moon in the sky. The swans could see the dark water far below. They were tired, yet they did not stop, but kept on flying. The old, strong swans led the way, with the younger and weaker ones following. A young swan was the last in line. Its strength was failing. It flapped its wings and felt it could not fly any farther. Then, spreading its wings, it sailed down, closer and closer to the water, while its comrades winged farther and farther away, becoming white spots in the moonlight. The swan settled on the water and folded its wings. The waves rocked it gently. Now the flock was like a tiny white streak in the light sky. The whistle of the swans' wings could barely be heard in the stillness. When they disappeared from view the swan threw back its neck and closed its eyes. It did not move. Only the sea, rising and falling, made the swan rise and dip as well. At dawn a light breeze rippled the water and some of it splashed against the swan's white breast. The swan opened its eyes. A red dawn was breaking in the east, while the moon and the stars had paled. The swan sighed, arched its neck, flapped its wings and rose up. Its wing-tips skimmed the water as it took to the air. The swan rose higher and higher, and when the water was far below it turned south, towards the warm lands. It flew on alone over the mysterious sea, following the direction its comrades had taken.

THE ELEPHANT

A man owned an elephant. He did not feed it properly and made it work hard. One day the elephant became angry and stepped on its master. The man died. Then his wife began to weep. She brought her children out to where the elephant was and tossed them at its feet, saying: "Elephant! You have killed their father. Now kill them, too." The elephant looked at the children, raised the eldest boy in its trunk and gently sat him on its back. From then on the elephant obeyed the boy and worked for him.

THE SPARROW AND THE SWALLOWS

One day I was out in the yard, looking at a swallow's nest under the eaves. As I watched, both swallows left the nest and flew away.

While they were away a sparrow flew down from the roof, hopped onto the edge of the nest, looked around and darted into the nest. Then it stuck its head out and chirped.

Soon after, one of the swallows returned. It wanted to enter the nest, but as soon as it saw the visitor it twittered, beat its wings and flew away.

The sparrow sat there, chirping.

All of a sudden a little flock of swallows appeared. Each swallow flew up to the nest, as though to have a look at the sparrow, and then flew off again.

The sparrow was not frightened. It turned its head this way and that and continued to chirp.

And again the swallows flew up to the nest, fussed about and flew off again.

There was a reason why the swallows were flying up to the nest: each brought a little glob of mud in its beak, and together they were gradually closing up the entrance to the nest.

Again and again they flew up and away, making the opening smaller and smaller as they added more and more mud to it.

At first, the sparrow's neck could be seen, then only its head, then its beak, and at last nothing at all could be seen. The swallows had closed it in the nest completely. Then they flew off and began circling over the house, whistling shrilly.

THE SEA EAGLE

A sea eagle built its nest by a road far from the sea and hatched its young.

One day some people were working by the tree. The eagle came flying back to its nest, carrying a large fish in its talons. The people saw the fish, surrounded the tree and began to shout and throw stones at the eagle.

The eagle dropped the fish. A man picked it up and the people went off.

The eagle perched on the edge of the nest. Its fledgelings raised their heads and began to cheep. They were begging for food.

The eagle was weary and could not fly to the sea again. It settled on the nest, spread its wings over the fledgelings, caressed them, preened their feathers and seemed to be asking them to wait a while. But the more it caressed them, the louder they cried.

Then the eagle flew off the nest and settled on the top branch of the tree.

The fledgelings cried still more piteously.

All of a sudden the eagle uttered a piercing cry, spread its wings and flew off heavily towards the sea.

It was far into the evening by the time the eagle returned. It was flying slowly and close to the ground. Once again it had a large fish in its talons.

When the eagle reached the tree it looked about to see whether there were not any people nearby again. Then it quickly folded its wings and perched on the edge of the nest.

The fledgelings raised their heads and opened their beaks, and the eagle tore the fish apart and fed its children.

THE SHARK

Our ship was at anchor near the African Coast. It was a fine day, with a fresh breeze blowing from the sea, but towards evening the weather changed: it became very close. Hot air from the Sakhara was rushing towards us as from a hot oven.

Shortly before sunset the captain came out on the bridge and shouted: "You may go swimming! " In no time some sailors had jumped into the water, lowered a sail and made it fast, to serve as a swimming pool.

There were two boys on board the ship. The boys were the first to dive in, but they felt cramped in the sail and so decided to have a race in the open sea.

Both cut through the water like salamanders as they swam to the spot where a barrel bobbed above the anchor.

One boy overtook the other at first, but then dropped behind. His father, an old gunner, stood on deck, watching his son with pride. But when the boy lagged behind, his father shouted, "Come on, now! "

All of a sudden someone on deck shouted: "A shark! " There in the water we all saw the monster's fin.

The shark was heading straight for the boys.

"Back! Back! Turn back! It's a shark! " the gunner shouted. But the boys did not hear him. They swam on, laughing and shouting more loudly than before.

The gunner was as pale as a sheet as he stood there motionlessly, staring at the boys.

The sailors lowered a boat, jumped into it and bent to their

oars. The boat streaked towards the boys. However, they were still far away, while the shark was now within fifty feet of them.

At first, the boys did not hear the men shouting, nor did they see the shark. But then one of them looked back, and we all heard his shriek. The boys began swimming away from each other.

The shriek seemed to have awakened the gunner. He dashed towards the cannons. He pointed the barrel of one, crouched, sighted, and picked up the portfire.

Everyone on board the ship froze, waiting to see what would follow.

The cannon boomed. We saw the gunner fall beside it and bury his face in his hands. We could not see what had happened to the shark or to the boys, for smoke screened all.

However, when the smoke lifted over the water there was a murmur from all sides. It grew louder until, finally, a joyous shout went up.

The old gunner uncovered his face, rose and looked down at the sea.

The yellow belly of the dead shark bobbed on the waves. A few minutes later the rowboat reached the boys and brought them back to the ship.

THE DIVE

A ship had sailed around the world and was returning home. It was a still day and everyone was on deck. A large monkey darted in and out among the crowd, amusing everyone. The monkey hopped, jumped, made funny faces and mimicked the people. One could see that it knew they enjoyed watching it, and this excited it still more.

The monkey jumped towards a twelve-year-old boy, the captain's son, tore his hat from his head, put it on and quickly scampered up the mast. Everyone laughed. The boy, now hatless, did not know whether to laugh or to cry.

The monkey sat down on the first yard, removed the hat and, using its hands and teeth, began tearing it. It seemed to be teasing the boy, pointing at him and making faces. The boy shook his fist at it and shouted, but this only made the monkey tear at the hat more viciously. The sailors laughed still louder, but the boy turned red, threw off his jacket and rushed up the mast after the monkey. In no time he had climbed the rigging to the first yard, but just as he was about to snatch his hat, the monkey, more nimble and quick than he, scampered higher.

"I'll get you! " the boy shouted and also climbed higher.

The monkey beckoned to him again and climbed higher yet, but the boy was so excited by now that he kept on after it. Thus, in no time, both the monkey and the boy reached the top of the mast. At the very top the monkey stretched out to its full length, grabbed hold of the rigging with the toes of one foot and hung the hat on the tip of the last yard. Then it climbed onto the top of the mast and bared its teeth in a happy grin. It was about four feet from the mast to the tip of the yard where the hat hung, and only by letting go of the rigging and the mast could it be reached.

But the boy was too excited. He let go of the mast and stepped out onto the yard. Everyone on deck had been watching and laughing at what had been going on between the monkey and the captain's son, but when they saw him let go of the rigging and place his foot on the yard, balancing with his outstretched arms, all stood still in terror.

Should he miss his step, he would fall to his death on deck. But even if he did not miss his step and reached the end of the yard and got his hat, it would be nearly impossible to turn

around and walk back to the mast. In silence everyone watched, waiting to see what would happen.

Suddenly someone on deck cried out in horror. The cry brought the boy to his senses. He looked down and began to teeter.

Just then his father, the captain, came out of his cabin. He had his gun on his arm, for he was going to shoot some gulls. He saw his son standing on the yard. In a flash he raised his gun, aimed at the boy and shouted:

"Into the water! Jump into the water this minute, or I'll shoot you! "

The boy teetered, but did not seem to understand.

"Jump, or I'll shoot you! One, two..." and just as his father shouted "three! ", the boy dived.

THE LION AND THE DOG

Once a dog happened to get into a lion's cage in the Zoo. The dog tucked its tail between its legs and crouched in a corner of the cage. The lion went up to it and sniffed at it.

The dog rolled over on its back and wagged its tail.

The lion nudged it with its paw and rolled it over.

The dog jumped up and then stood on its hind legs.

The lion looked at the dog, cocked its head this way and that, and did not touch it.

When the keeper tossed the lion a chunk of meat, the lion tore off a piece and left it for the dog.

That evening, when the lion lay down to sleep, the dog lay down beside it and rested its head on the lion's paw.

From that day on the dog lived in the lion's cage. The lion acted friendly towards it. It slept beside the dog and sometimes played with it.

Thus the lion and the dog shared a cage for a whole year.

At the end of the year the dog took sick and died. The lion refused to eat. It sniffed at the dog, licked it and nudged it with its paw.

When the lion realised that the dog was dead it reared up, bristled, lashed its tail against its sides, rushed at the walls of the cage and gnawed at the lock and at the floorboards.

All that day the lion thrashed about in the cage and roared. Then it lay down beside the dead dog and became still. The keeper wanted to take the dead dog away, but the lion would not let him near it.

The keeper thought the lion would forget its loss if it were given another dog, and so another dog was let into the cage. But the lion rushed at it and killed it instantly. Then it lay down beside the dead dog, put its paws around it and remained thus for five days.

On the sixth day the lion died.

Alexander Kuprin

THE ELEPHANT

I

A little girl was ill. Each day the doctor, Mikhail Petrovich, whom she had known for a very, very long time, came to see her. Sometimes, there were two other doctors with him whom she did not know. They would turn her on her stomach and then on her back, listening for something, their ears pressed to her body, pulling down her eyelids and looking. All the while their faces were very stern, and they made important huffing sounds, and spoke to each other in a strange tongue.

Then they would leave the nursery and go into the parlour, where her mother awaited them. The most important-looking doctor, a tall, grey-haired man in gold-rimmed eyeglasses, spoke to her for a long time in a very serious tone. The door was not shut, and so the girl could see and hear everything from her bed. There was much she could not understand, but she knew they were talking about her. Her mother looked at the doctor from her large, tired eyes that were red from weeping. In parting, the doctor said in a loud voice:

"Try to see that she is never bored, and fulfil her every wish."

"Oh, doctor! That's just it! She doesn't want anything!"

"Hm... Well then, try to think of what she used to like before she became ill. Some toys ... or sweets...."

"Doctor, she doesn't want anything."

"Then try to arouse her interest in something.... Try anything.... Take my word for it, if you are able to make her laugh, to be happy, it will be the very best medicine. You must understand that your daughter's illness is simply an indifference to life, and nothing more. Good-day, Madame."

II

"Darling, isn't there anything you'd like? Tell me, Nadya," her mother said.

"No, Mamma, I don't want anything."

"Would you like me to bring you all your dolls? We can put the little armchairs, the sofa, the table and the tea set on your bed. The dolls will have tea and talk about the weather and their children's health."

"Thank you, Mamma... But I don't want them... I'm so bored...."

"All right, dear, we won't play dolls. Would you like me to call Katya or Zhenya? They're your best friends."

"No, don't, Mamma. Please, don't. There's not anything I want at all. Oh, I'm so bored!"

"Would you like a bar of chocolate?"

But the girl did not reply. She just stared sadly at the ceiling. Nothing hurt her. She did not even have a fever, but she was getting thinner and weaker with each passing day. She did not care what was done to her, and did not wish for anything. She simply lay in her bed day and night, quietly and sadly. At times she would doze off for half an hour, but even her dreams were of something long, grey and as mournful as the rain in autumn.

When the door from the nursery to the parlour was left open, and the door from the parlour to the study, too, the girl could see her father. Papa kept pacing up and down, smoking one cigarette after another. Sometimes he would come into the nursery, sit down on the edge of the bed and stroke Nadya's feet gently. Then he would suddenly get up and go over to the window. He would whistle a tune as he looked out at the street, but his shoulders would be convulsed. Then he would hastily press his handkerchief first to one eye and then to the other and would go off to his study, as if he were cross. There he would begin pacing up and down again, smoking cigarette after cigarette.... His study would become fairly blue from all the smoke.

III

One morning the little girl was a bit more cheerful than usual when she awoke. She had dreamed about something, but couldn't remember what it was, and so gazed long and intently into her mother's eyes.

"Is there anything you'd like?" her mother asked.

Suddenly the girl remembered her dream and said in a whisper, as if it were a secret:

"Mamma ... can I have an ... elephant? But I don't mean a picture of one. Can I?"

"Certainly you can, darling. By all means."

Her mother went off into the study and told Papa that Nadya wanted an elephant. Papa quickly put on his hat and coat and left the house. Half an hour later he returned with a lovely, expensive toy. It was a large grey elephant which nodded its head and swished its tail. There was a red cloth on the elephant's back and on it a gold canopied seat with three little men.

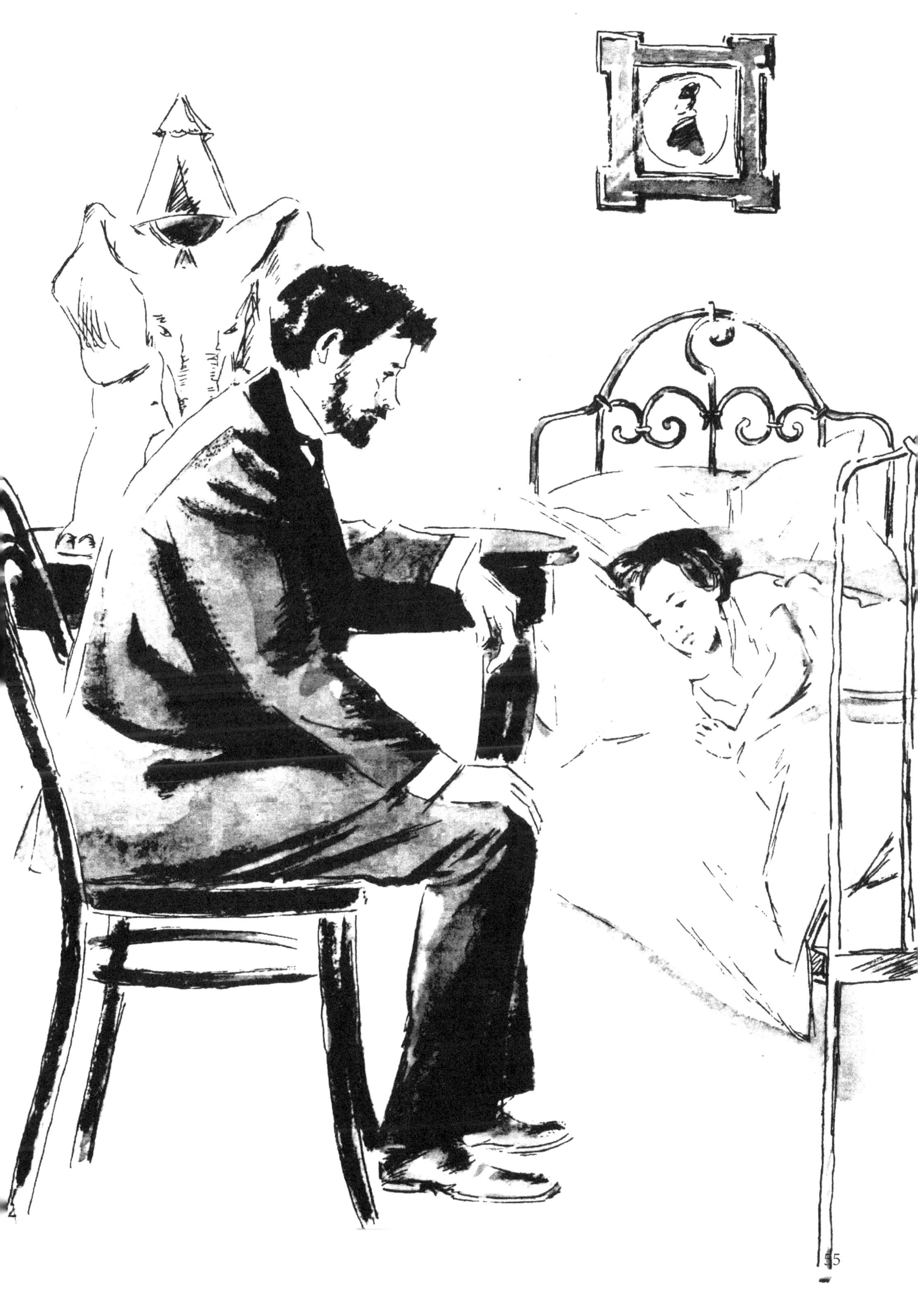

But the girl looked at the toy as indifferently as she did at the ceiling and the walls, and her voice when she spoke was listless.

"No. That's not what I meant at all. I wanted a real, live elephant, but this one is dead."

"Wait a minute, Nadya," Papa said. "I'll wind it up, and it will be just like a real, live one."

He wound up the elephant with a little key, and it nodded its head and swished its tail as it began to move its feet and walk slowly across the table. The girl was not at all interested. In fact, she was bored, but she did not want to disappoint her father and so whispered obediently:

"Thank you ever so much, dear Papa. I don't think anyone I know has such a lovely toy. But.... Remember, long ago, you promised to take me to the animal circus to see a real elephant ... and you never did."

"But, darling, try to understand that this is quite out of the question. An elephant is very big. It's as tall as the ceiling and can't fit into our house.... Besides, where will I find one?"

"Oh, I don't need such a big one, Papa. A little one will be just as good, as long as it's alive. Even if it's only this big.... Even a teeny-weeny one."

"My sweet, I'd do anything for you, but this is something I can't do. Why, it's just the same as if you'd suddenly said: 'Reach up and get me the sun from the sky, Papa.' "

She smiled sadly.

"You're so silly, Papa. Don't you think I know you can't get the sun, because it'll burn you! Or the moon, either. Oh, I wish I had a baby elephant ... a real one."

She closed her eyes and whispered, "I'm so tired ... Don't be angry at me, Papa...."

Her father clapped his hands to his head and rushed off to his study. She could see him pacing about there for a while. Then he threw his half-finished cigarette to the floor (something Mamma always scolded him for) and shouted to the maid:

"Get my hat and coat, Olga!"

His wife followed him to the foyer and asked: "Where are you going, Sasha?"

He was breathing hard as he buttoned up his coat.

"I don't know myself.... But I think I'll really bring back a live elephant today."

His wife looked at him anxiously. "Are you well, dear? Do you have a headache? Perhaps you did not sleep well?"

"I did not sleep at all," he replied crossly. "I see you'd like to ask me whether I'm insane. Not yet. Goodbye. Everything should be settled by this evening."

The front door banged loudly, and he was gone.

IV

Two hours later he was in a front-row seat at the animal circus, watching the trained animals perform for their master. The clever dogs jumped, turned somersaults, danced, howled to music and spelled out words with large cardboard letters. The monkeys, some of which had on red skirts and others blue trousers, walked across a tightrope and rode a large poodle. Huge tawny lions jumped through burning hoops. A lum bering seal fired a pistol. The elephants were in the last act. There were three of them: one large elephant and two very small, midget elephants, although each was bigger than a horse. It was strange to see these huge animals, so clumsy and awkward to look at, perform the most difficult tricks which even a very agile person would never be able to do. The biggest elephant was the most clever of the three. It first stood up on its hind legs, then sat down, stood on its head with its feet in the air, walked over wooden bottles, walked on a rolling barrel, turned the pages of a large cardboard book with its trunk and, finally, sat down at a table, having first tied a napkin round its neck, and ate its dinner just like a well-mannered child.

Soon the show was over. The audience was leaving. Nadya's father went up to the roly-poly German owner of the animal circus. He was standing in his box with a large black cigar clenched between his teeth.

"I beg your pardon," Nadya's father said. "Would you agree to letting your elephant come to my house for a short while?"

The German's eyes grew wide. He gaped, and the cigar fell out of his mouth. He bent over with a grunt, picked it up and stuck it back into his

mouth. Only then did he say, "Let you have the elephant? To take home? I don't understand what you mean."

You could see by the man's expression that he also felt like asking Nadya's father whether he had a headache.... But the father hastily explained the situation: his only daughter, Nadya, had a very strange illness which the doctors themselves could not even diagnose properly. She had been bedridden for a month and was getting thinner and losing strength with each passing day. She took no interest in anything, she was bored by everything and was wasting away. The doctors said she was to be entertained, but nothing pleased her; they said her every wish was to be carried out, but she did not wish for anything. Today she had asked to see a real, live elephant. Was this really so impossible?

Then he added in a tremorous voice, as he took hold of the button on the German's coat: "You see ... I certainly hope my child gets well. But ... but ... what if her illness progresses ... and she dies?... Just think: to the

end of my days I'll torture myself with the thought that I did not carry out her last wish, her very last wish!"

The German frowned and scratched his left eyebrow absently with his pinky. Finally, he said, "How old is your daughter?"

"Six."

"Hm... My Liza is also six.... But it will be very expensive. The elephant will have to be brought to your house at night and taken back the next night. It can't be done in the daytime. The public will gather and a big scandal is sure to follow.... So, this means I lose a whole day's earnings, and you will have to cover my losses."

"Oh, certainly. By all means. Don't worry about that."

"Now, will the police let me take the elephant into the house?"

"I'll arrange it. They will."

"One more question: will your landlord let the elephant be taken into your house?"

"Yes. The house is mine."

"Ah! That's fine. Now, one more question: what floor are you on?"

"The second."

"Hm... That's not so good. Does your house have a wide staircase, a high ceiling, a large room, wide doors and a very strong floor? Because my Tommy is nine feet four inches high and fifteen and a half feet long. Besides, he weighs close to a ton."

Nadya's father was silent for a moment.

"You know what?" he said. "Let's go to my house now and examine everything on the spot. If need be, I'll have the doorways widened."

"Good!" said the circus owner.

V

That night the elephant was taken to visit the sick child.

He walked proudly down the middle of the street in its white robe, nodding its head and curling and uncurling its trunk. Despite the late hour, a large crowd followed him. However, the elephant paid no attention to this, for he was used to seeing hundreds of people at the show every day. He only became a bit angry once, when a street urchin ran right up to him and began making faces and hopping about to amuse the idlers.

At this, the elephant calmly lifted the boy's cap with his trunk and tossed it over a fence that had nails sticking up all along the top.

A policeman entered the crowd and pleaded, "Please disperse, everybody. What's so unusual about this? Hmph! As if you'd never seen a live elephant in the streets before."

They approached the house. All the doors leading to the dining room, beginning with the front door, were wide open, for all the latches had been hammered back.

However, the elephant stopped when he came to the staircase. He stood there anxiously and would not go on.

"You have to give him something sweet," the circus owner said. "A sweet bun or something.... Come on, Tommy! Hey, boy!"

Nadya's father ran off to the nearby bakery and bought a large round pistachio cake. The elephant was quite prepared to swallow it whole,

together with the cardboard box, but the owner only gave him a quarter. Tommy liked the taste of it and stretched his trunk out for another chunk. But his owner was too clever for him. He held the cake in his outstretched hand as he backed up the stairs, with the elephant having to follow, his trunk reaching out, his ears flapping. Tommy was given another chunk on the landing.

In this way he was led into the dining room. All the furniture had already been taken out, and a thick layer of straw covered the floor. The elephant's leg was tied to a ring that had been screwed into the floor. Fresh carrots, cabbage and turnips were set out in front of him. His owner lay down on a sofa nearby. Then the lights were put out and everyone went to sleep.

VI

The little girl awoke at dawn the next day. The first thing she said was: "Where's the elephant? Did he come?"

"Yes," her mother replied. "But he said Nadya was to wash first, and then to have a soft-boiled egg and a cup of hot milk."

"Is he good?"

"Yes, very. Eat, dear. We'll go in to see him right now."

"Is he funny-looking?"

"Rather. Put on your warm sweater."

The egg was quickly eaten, the milk was drunk. Nadya was put in the pram she used to be wheeled around in when she was still too little to walk and was taken into the dining room.

The elephant was much bigger than Nadya had expected from seeing a picture of one. He was just a tiny bit lower than the doorway and took up half the dining room in length. His skin was very coarse and fell in heavy folds. His feet were as thick as posts. His long tail had a brush on the very end. There were big bumps on his head. His drooping ears were huge and looked like burdocks. His eyes were tiny, but intelligent and kind. His tusks had been sawed off. His trunk was like a long snake and ended in two nostrils with a movable lobe like a finger at the tip. If the elephant had stretched his trunk out to its full length, he would have probably touched the window.

The girl was not frightened in the least. She was simply a little awed by his great size. However, her nurse, sixteen-year-old Polya, was terrified and began to scream.

The elephant's owner went over to Nadya and said, "Good morning, Miss. Don't be afraid. Tommy is very good and likes children."

The girl offered the German her small, pale hand. "How do you do?" she said. "I'm not frightened at all. What's his name?"

"Tommy."

"How do you do, Tommy," she said and nodded. "Did you sleep well?"

She offered him her hand, too. The elephant took it carefully and pressed her small, slim fingers with his strong, flexible one and did this much more gently than Mikhail Petrovich, the doctor. At the same time, the elephant nodded his head, and his little eyes became slits, as if they were laughing.

"He understands everything, doesn't he?" the girl said to the German.

"Absolutely everything, Miss."

"It's just that he can't talk, isn't it?"

"Yes, that's it. He can't talk. You know, I have an only daughter, too, and she's just as big as you. Her name is Liza. Tommy and she are very good friends. The best of friends."

"Have you had your tea yet, Tommy?" the girl asked the elephant.

The elephant stretched out his trunk again and blew a strong stream of warm air into the girl's face, making her silky hair fly up.

Nadya laughed and clapped her hands. The German guffawed.

He was as big and fat and kind as an elephant, and Nadya thought there was a resemblance between them. Perhaps he and Tommy were related?

"No, he hasn't had his tea yet, Miss. But he'd really enjoy some sugar-water. He also loves buns."

A tray of buns was brought in. The girl offered one to the elephant. He curled his finger over it quickly, and his trunk carried it up, tucking it someplace under his head, where he had a funny-looking, triangular, hairy under-lip. Nadya could hear the bun scratching against his dry skin. Tommy did the same with a second bun, and a third one, and a fourth one, and a fifth one. He nodded his head in thanks, and his little eyes became still smaller slits from pleasure. The girl laughed happily.

When all the buns were gone, Nadya introduced the elephant to her dolls, saying, "See, Tommy, this pretty doll is Sonya. She's a very kind child, but she won't eat her soup. This is Natasha, Sonya's daughter. She's just starting her lessons, but knows most of the alphabet. And this is

Matryoshka. She was my very first doll. See, she's lost her nose, and her head's glued on, and she hasn't any hair left. But I can't send the old thing away, can I, Tommy? she used to be Sonya's mother, but now she's our cook. Come on, let's play. You'll be the papa, Tommy, and I'll be the mamma, and these will be our children."

Tommy agreed. He laughed, took Matryoshka by the neck and lifted the doll to his mouth. But it was only for fun. He chewed it a bit and put it back in the girl's lap, although it was now rather wet and slightly crumpled.

Then Nadya showed him a big picture book and said, "This is a horse, this is a canary, this is a rifle.... Here's a bird in a cage, here's a pail, a mirror, a stove, a spade, a crow.... Look! Here's an elephant! It's not at all like one, is it? Elephants are never this small, are they, Tommy?"

Tommy agreed that elephants never were that small. In fact, he didn't like the picture one bit. He lifted the edge of the page with his finger and turned it over.

Soon it was time for dinner, but it was impossible to get Nadya away from the elephant. The elephant's owner came to the rescue and said, "Wait. We'll settle things nicely. They'll have their dinner together."

He told the elephant to sit down. The elephant sat down obediently, making the floor tremble, the dishes rattle in the cupboard and the plaster come off the ceiling in the room below. The girl sat down opposite him. The table was placed between them. A tablecloth was tied around the elephant's neck, and the new friends began to eat their dinner. The girl had a bowl of chicken soup and a cutlet, while the elephant had a pile of raw vegetables and salad. The girl was given a tiny glass of sherry, and the elephant some warm water with a glass of rum in it. He drew the liquid up into his trunk from the bowl with relish. Then there was dessert: a cup of cocoa for the girl and half a cake for the elephant. This time it was a nut cake. All the while the German and the girl's father were in the study, where the German was drinking beer with great pleasure.

After dinner some of her father's friends dropped in. While still in the foyer, they were told of the elephant in the house so that they would not be frightened. At first, they did not believe it, but then, catching sight of Tommy, they huddled together in the doorway.

"Don't be afraid! He's very good," the girl said to calm them.

Nevertheless, they quickly passed into the parlour, stayed but a few minutes and left.

Evening drew near. It was getting late and time for the little girl to go to bed, but it was impossible to get her away from the elephant. She finally fell asleep beside him and was carried back into the nursery. She did not even know she was being put to bed.

That night Nadya dreamed that she married Tommy and that they had many children, all of them jolly little elephants. The elephant was taken back to the circus that night. He, too, dreamed of the sweet, lovely girl. Besides, he dreamed of nut cakes as big as the carriage gate.

The next morning the little girl awoke in the best of spirits and as before, when she had been healthy, she shouted in a loud, impatient voice for all to hear:

"I want my milk!"

When her mother heard her she hurried in joyously.

The little girl suddenly recalled everything that had happened the day before and said: "But where's Tommy?"

Her mother explained that he had to go home to attend to his affairs, because he had children who could not be left alone, but that he had sent his regards to Nadya and had said that he was expecting her to visit him as soon as she got well.

The little girl smiled mischievously and said, "Tell Tommy that I'm all well now!"

www.ingramcontent.com/pod-product-compliance
Lightning Source LLC
LaVergne TN
LVHW080555160826
845677LV00010B/1867

* 9 7 8 9 3 9 0 3 5 5 5 3 2 *